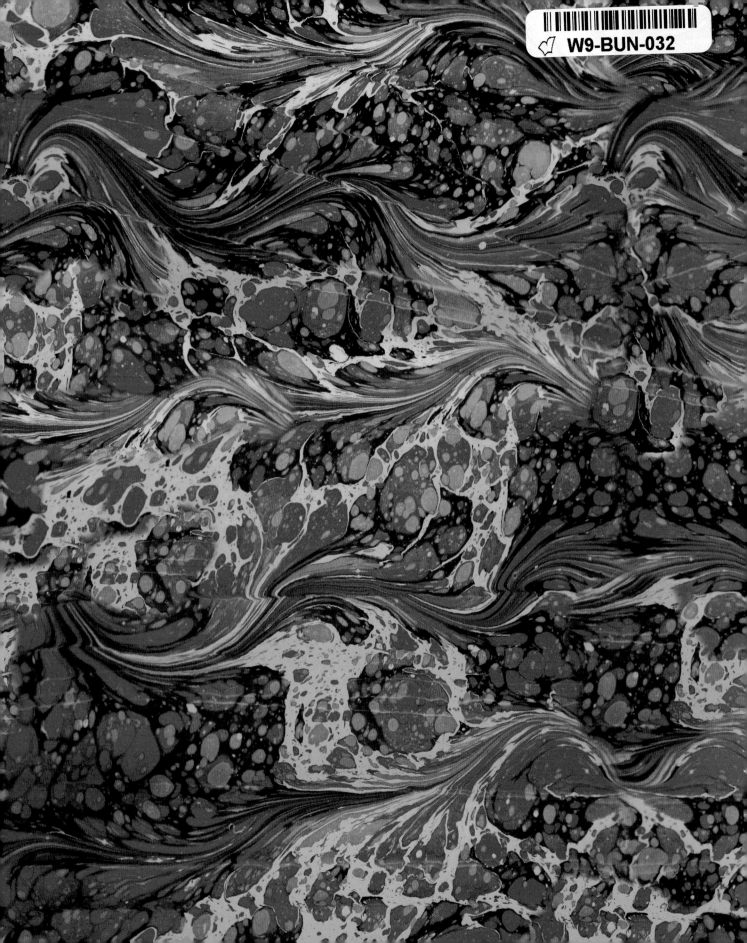

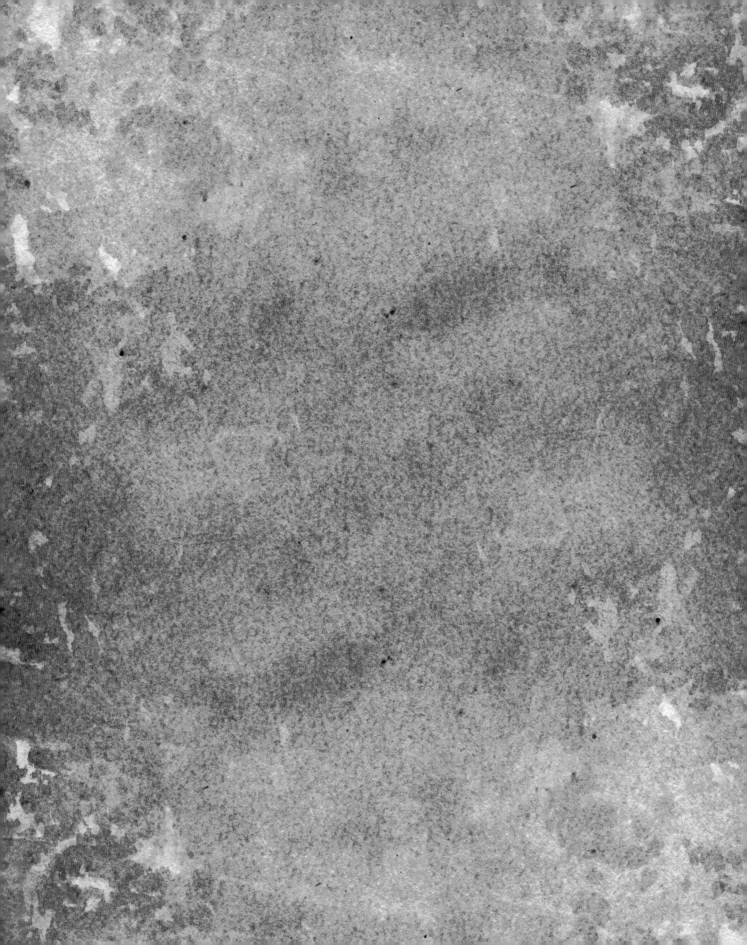

Bear CRIMBO

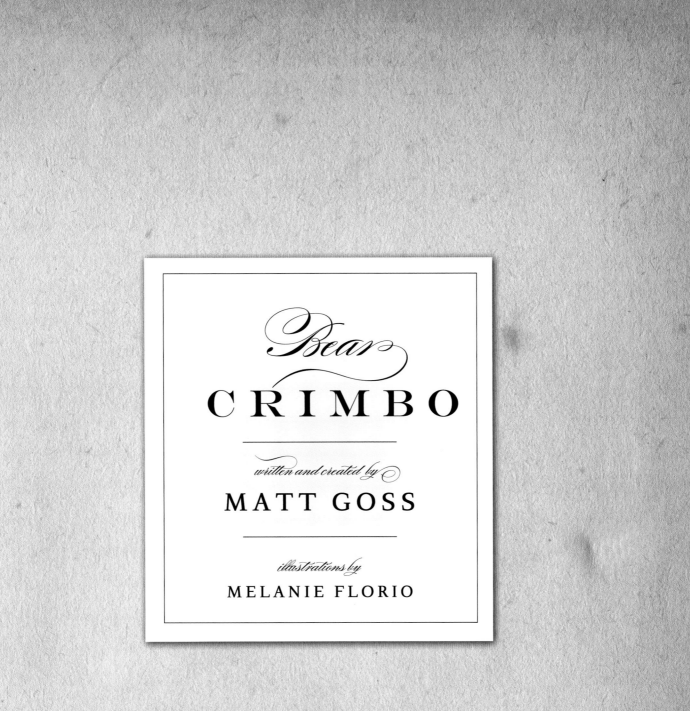

Bear

CRIMBO

written and created by

MATT GOSS

illustrations by

MELANIE FLORIO

HILTON
PUBLISHING

BEAR CRIMBO lives at Number 32, Plip Plop Road, in the loft of Mr. and Mrs. Flump's house. Bear Crimbo's three best friends are Rita Robin, Bobby Spider, and Alfie Mouse, who share the cozy little loft they all call home.

Every day, Bear Crimbo takes great care to make sure his crisp, white shirt and little old tweed jacket are just perfect. Rita and Alfie call Bear Crimbo "B. C." They really are the best of friends.

It was December 20th, and Alfie Mouse and Rita Robin knew only too well what that meant: every year, on exactly the same day, Bear Crimbo became completely obsessed with meeting Santa. "La, la, la-la . . ." sang Bear Crimbo. "You'll never guess what day it is," he said.

"No," they replied.

"December 20th!" he shouted. And even before Alfie and Rita could pretend to be surprised, Bear Crimbo cried out, "I must meet Santa!"

But then, with his head in his big paws, he softly whispered, "Maybe Santa doesn't listen to bears."

"That's not true," chirped Robin. "Santa can hear everyone."

"Santa never hears me, and I'm always a good bear."

In their hearts Rita and Alfie knew that it would be very difficult, maybe even impossible, for Bear Crimbo to meet Santa. But Alfie Mouse responded with authority: "I personally guarantee that this will be the year you will finally get to tell Santa what you want for Christmas."

"Really?" Bear Crimbo asked, wide-eyed.

"Yes, there is not a doubt in my mousy mind," said Alfie.

Bear Crimbo started to sing, "I'm going to meet Santa, I'm going to meet Santa." But then, mid-song, he asked, "How?"

"Er, er, er," stuttered Alfie Mouse, looking at Rita for help.

Then, calmly, Rita Robin said, "A letter."

"But I've . . . I've already sent so many letters . . . and Santa never replies," said Bear Crimbo.

"But this letter will be different, B. C.," Rita assured him, "because this time I will personally fly it to Santa."

Silence covered the loft. "B. C. has fainted!" squeaked Alfie Mouse.

He ran and filled a sewing thimble with rainwater and splashed Bear Crimbo's face.

Cough, cough, splutter!

As Bear Crimbo awoke, he said, breathless with excitement, "I've just had an amazing dreamy where Rita said she was going to fly my lovely letter to Santa."

"That wasn't a dreamy, B.C.," said Rita. "I said it, and I meant it. So start writing your lovely letter; we only have five days."

Bear Crimbo was amazed, excited, nervous, even a little scared. He couldn't believe that Santa would finally get one of his letters. Santa might even reply to it!

BEAR CRIMBO WRITES HIS LETTER

Crimbo stood up and said, "This will be the loveliest letter ever." Then, with a feather pen and fresh ink made from blueberries and rainwater, Bear Crimbo started to write.

Seconds turned into minutes,
minutes into much morey minutes,
and much morey minutes into hours.

By 3 A-Emily in the morning, Alfie Mouse was asleep in Bear Crimbo's jacket pocket and Rita Robin lay next to the warm beeswax candle that glowed upon Bear Crimbo's lovely letter.

Cock-a-doodle-doo!

Alfie Mouse had already been up for over an hour, in Mrs. Flump's kitchen, getting biscuits and bread ready for Rita Robin's long journey to see Santa.

Bear Crimbo nervously handed his lovely letter to Rita. She smiled and said, "Don't worry, B. C., it's all going to be just fine, but we do need to make your lovely letter water-proofy. I have asked for the help of Bobby Spider."

"Alright, you lot," said Bobby Spider suddenly. "Nice to meet you, nice to meet you . . ." Bobby Spider shook Bear Crimbo's hand with all eight of his hands. Bobby Spider always made Bear Crimbo laugh, because Bobby couldn't help saying "nice to meet you," even if you had seen him only an hour ago.

Rita explained that Bobby had agreed to cover Bear Crimbo's lovely letter in his finest silk. "Making it completely water-proofy," Bobby Spider chimed in, "and nice to meet you, nice to meet you."

Bear Crimbo tried not to giggle. "I am so grateful for your generosity," he said, "and for the use of your finest silk, and it's nice to meet you too, Bobby Spider."

"I hope you don't mind," said Alfie Mouse, "but I have taken the liberty of borrowing this beautiful sequiny purse I found in Mr. and Mrs. Flump's closet."

As Bobby Spider was busy weaving away in the corner, Alfie Mouse and Bear Crimbo carefully lay the tiny strap over Rita Robin's shoulder.

At that moment, the calm was broken with the words "Nice to meet you, nice to meet you, all done, completely water-proofy, oh, yes, and nice to meet you." The whole loft was filled with laughter.

After a few much morey hours, the day settled into the loft. Alfie Mouse was the first to speak. "We must hurry," he exclaimed. "It's top of the clock already!"

That's twelve o'clock in people time.

Rita Robin had never flown after dark. She put her wings around Alfie Mouse and Bear Crimbo and said softly, "Light the big beeswax candle on the window sill to guide me home safely."

Alfie Mouse tried to be strong, but he couldn't help wiping a tear that had fallen onto his little wet nose. Bear Crimbo was anxious too, suddenly faced with the thought of being separated from one of his best friends in the whole world for more than once around the clock.

With all of his heart, he said to Rita, "Please don't go. Please don't."

Rita replied softly, "That's what best friends are for. In all the years we have known each other, you have never asked me for anything—and this is something I want to do for you."

With that said and the water-proofy, silk-bound lovely letter safely in the sequiny purse, Rita kissed them both and was gone.

Rita's Flight

Although Rita was a superhero to Bear Crimbo and Alfie Mouse, her heart tingled with fear. But the thought of Santa reading Bear Crimbo's lovely letter filled her with so much pride that she flew like a bright red arrow non-stop for two times around the clock, without food or water, fueled just by friendship.

Rita Robin passed ships, trains, skyscrapers, wild horses, mountains, and even some dogs that barked good-luck. She continued to fly well into the second day and eventually came upon the Lazy Forest, where everything moved so slowly.

The Lazy Forest is definitely a very scary place! As the day moved on, the sun began to give in to rain, and each drop that fell on Rita's feathers made a little sound: tip top, tip top, tip, tip, top. Rita knew that she must find a safe, warm place to sleep. Fortunately, she was near the Emerald River, where an old friend, Harry the Bassett Hound, lived.

Harry wasn't like most dogs. He never chewed on bones, and he lived with cats. And he was a vegetarian, which means he didn't eat meat. He loved one thing more than anything—honey. Yes, sticky, sweet HONEY. Everyone loved Harry, especially the bees. All he had to say was, "Bees, if you please," and they would bring Harry his daily supply of honey.

When Harry saw Rita, he was happier than happy itself. As the sun fell asleep so the moon could watch over them, Rita told the bees, cats, and Harry the Bassett Hound the reason for her journey. When she was done with her story, the

bees lit a candle to keep her warm, and, with the sound of crickets singing, Rita thought of her three best friends.

Meanwhile, back at Mr. and Mrs. Flump's loft, Bear Crimbo and Alfie Mouse asked the moon and the stars to keep Rita safe. The second that Rita fell asleep in Harry Hound's house all those miles away, as if there were a magic connection between the three friends, Alfie climbed into Bear Crimbo's jacket pocket and they both drifted off into the land of dreamies.

THE EMERALD RIVER

As the sun kissed the horizon, and the dewdrops sparkled like a never-ending diamond necklace, the Emerald River glowed as green as an apple. Rita's new birdie friends started to sing softly; they knew she only had four days left before Christmas morning.

Just as things could not get more beautiful, Harry Hound made the loudest burp.

"Good morning," laughed Rita.

"It's all the honey," said Harry sheepishly. "It makes me . . . BURP!!"

After much morey minutes of laughing, Rita took a little dip on the edge of

Legend has it that if you look too long into the Emerald River, the beauty of the jewels is so powerful that they will never let you leave.

But the only thing on Rita's mind was Bear Crimbo's lovely letter held safely inside the little sequiny purse that had not left her side. The bees filled an acorn with honey to give Rita extra energy for her long journey. Rita quickly drank the honey, gave every-one a big hug, and was off on her way to the North Pole.

the Emerald River.

Back at the loft in Plip Plop Road, Bear Crimbo and Alfie Mouse had a problem: the candle on the window sill to guide Rita Robin home safely had already burned half-way down, and it had only been alight for one night. Bear Crimbo knew in his heart that the candle could only make it through one more once around the clock, P-Emily time. Alfie paced around and around the dusty loft, so much so that there was a perfect polished circle on the wooden floor where his big fluffy paws had been walking.

RITA MAKES A NEW FRIEND

The further Rita Robin flew north, the colder it became. The sun shone, but the wind blew so hard it could freeze the sea solid. For little Rita, the harder she flew, the slower she went. The sequiny purse was getting heavy with ice. Tiny little tears froze upon Rita's cheeks as she realized she could not make it to Santa's Grotto alone. To make things worse, the sun was feeling sleepy, so she had to find shelter quickly before the moon made everything blue.

Rita spotted the opening of a small cave on the edge of a snow-covered mountain, and she swooped—exhausted—into the dark place. Sadness filled her heart. As she lay down, more tears fell like tiny diamonds, each one making its own individual note as it landed on the cold, dark floor of the empty cave. But then, from out of the dark, Rita heard a SNAP!

She had never been more frightened in her life. She slowly looked behind her, holding her breath, and saw two dark brown eyes, two hundred times taller than she was. Rita let out the loudest scream and said, "Please don't eat me! There's nothing of me. I'm not even an appetizer."

At that very moment, an even louder scream came from the monster. "A talking bird! Help, help me, a talking bird!" Then, in the moonlight, Rita could see that it wasn't a monster after all. It was just a big—no, not big—a big, massive, white fluffy bear.

Back at Plip Plop Road, it was 2 A-Emily in the morning and Bear Crimbo sat waiting anxiously for Rita on the window sill. He imagined Rita laughing and joking with Santa and all his helpers, comparing her red feathers with Santa's reindeer's bright red nose. Little did Bear Crimbo know that Rita was actually sitting with a bear fifty times taller than himself. Bear Crimbo only knew that the candle had no more than two or three much morey hours left.

GETTING TO KNOW T. J.

Rita's day had still not come to an end. She had just spent two much morey hours trying to convince the big, fluffy bear that all birds *can* talk.

"Well, they never talk to me," he said.

"Well, do you ever talk to them?" she asked.

"Er, er, no . . ."

"Well," said Rita, "don't you think that might be the problem? Why don't you just say 'good morning' or 'hello' or 'I'm not going to eat you'?"

"What!" roared the bear. "I don't eat birds. I only eat pancakes."

Rita laughed so hard! Then she straightened out her feathers and said, "I'm Rita Robin, and it's very nice to meet you."

"My name is Thomas Jeffrey Wee Bonny Rufus James the First, or you can just call me T. J."

"Well, it's nice to meet you, T. J."

"It's nice to meet you too, Rita Robin." T. J. motioned with his paw. "Come this way," he said softly. As they walked down a dark tunnel, a soft warm light waited at the end for them. "Welcome to my home," said T. J. proudly.

Rita could not believe her eyes. In front of her was an old ship that must have been abandoned by pirates many years ago. T. J. had his very own private pirate mansion!

She spent the next few much morey hours telling T. J. about her long journey and how sad she felt that she would not be able to fulfill the promise she had made to Bear Crimbo.

"Listen," said T. J., "I don't know Crimbo, but he is a bear, right? Well, you're a friend of a bear, which makes you a friend of mine. I have to tell you something. You can definitely get Crimbo's lovely letter to Santa before Christmas!"

"How?" asked Rita.

"I can take it there for you," said T. J. "I know where Santa's Grotto is."

Rita said nothing. She just laid her head on an old pillow. In her mind, she thanked the stars and the moon, and sleepy time took her gently to the land of dreamies.

She woke the next morning to the sounds of shouts in the distance. "Hello! My name is T. J.," called the bear. "I am not going to eat you. Hello! Hello!" She made her way toward the entrance of the cave and found T. J. surrounded by about fifty birds of every shape and size, all talking at once. She let out a little giggle, and T. J. turned around with the biggest smile on his face. He sat down on a rock with a big thump, and Rita flew onto his arm.

"There have been so many times that I have been very lonely," said T. J., "and wished that I could talk to all the birdie birds that fly by my home, but I always thought that they couldn't talk. You, Rita Robin, have taught me that a simple 'hello' means everything." He leaned closer to Rita and whispered in her tiny ear, "I have invited all the birdies for Christmas dinner—

PANCAKES ALL AROUND!"

ALFIE'S DISCOVERY

Back at the loft of Plip Plop Road, the candle had burned down and gone out. Bear Crimbo and Alfie Mouse just sat there looking at the puff of smoke in disbelief.

"Nice to meet you, nice to meet you," Bobby Spider rattled on. "What's with the long faces? . . . Oh, the candle." Bobby scratched his chin eight times with each one of his hands, then he smiled. "Don't worry," he said. "I know how to guide Rita home safely." With that, he fired his web into a nearby tree, shouted, "Wah-hoo!" and was gone.

Alfie Mouse decided to go down to Mrs. Flump's kitchen for some biscuits and cheese. It was Mrs. Flump's little secret; she always left snacks for Alfie. She never saw him, but it was a special part of her day as much as his. The Flumps really were lovely people. When he got downstairs, Alfie Mouse saw Mrs. Flump through a little crack in the wall. She was reading letters—and they all said the same thing, that they wanted to meet Santa and they only wanted one thing for Christmas.

"There's no letter from Bear Crimbo this year," said Mrs. Flump to Mr. Flump.

At that moment, Alfie Mouse realized that Bear

Crimbo must have sneaked down the stairs

every year and placed his lovely letter by

Mr. and Mrs. Flump's front door for

the postman to take with him. None

of the letters had stamps on them.

Alfie Mouse realized that not one

of Crimbo's lovely letters had

ever left Plip Plop Road.

Alfie hoped, now more than ever, that Rita would be able to get Bear Crimbo's lovely letter to Santa. Alfie Mouse ran back upstairs with the little nubby snacks he had gathered. Bear Crimbo had just finished making a pot of tea; it was just the thing to pass the time while Bobby Spider finished his plan.

$\mathcal{R}$ITA AND T. J.

Rita looked up from the pancake she had only nibbled on. With sad eyes, she said, "If you do get the letter to Santa and if he does read it and if he goes to see Bear Crimbo, I won't be there to see such a wonderful moment. I am three days away from Plip Plop Road, and Christmas is only a day away. It's impossible for me to be home for Christmas morning."

T. J. sat there with a big smile on his face and with three pancakes hanging from his sharp, white teeth. "The reason you stopped here last night," he said, "was because you were not strong enough to fly against the wind, no matter how hard you flew. That's because the wind from the North Pole is the strongest wind in the world. But if you fly *with* it and lift up your tail to catch the Tail Wind, you can fly as fast as a rocket. You can use the strength, power, and speed of the Great North Wind to take you home in time for Christmas!" Rita was so delighted she flew up to T. J.'s face and hugged him as hard as she could.

But Rita knew she must leave soon to make it home in time, even with the help of the Great North Wind. She handed T. J. the sequiny purse that held Bear

Crimbo's lovely letter and said softly, "This is the most valuable thing I have ever been given. You are a good friend, and I cannot wait to tell B. C., Alfie, and Bobby about you. Do your best, and don't put yourself in harm's way, okay?"

Rita gave T. J. one last hug. Then she took a big run and shot out of the cave, straight up as high as she could possibly fly. And then she lifted her tail, opened her wings, and WHOOSH! She caught the Tail Wind and flew just like a rocket on her way home.

T. J.'s journey didn't start with quite as much excitement; he simply hung the sequiny purse from one of his big, sharp teeth and started to walk to Santa's Grotto, against the Great North Wind. Thomas Jeffery Wee Bonny Rufus James the First was a big white bear with an even bigger heart, so not even the Great North Wind was a match for him.

Bobby Spider's Plan

Back at Plip Plop Road, Bear Crimbo poured three cups of tea and waited to hear Bobby Spider's idea.

"Okay, okay," said Bobby, "first things first. I am going to cover the whole house in my finest silk—even the chimney. Then I'm going to cover every single tree in Plip Plop Road—yeah, the leaves and everything. Good plan? Yes, it's a good plan, nice to meet you—then I'm going to cover Alfie and B. C. in so much silk. I'm going to make a big ball of my finest silk and a giant web, then I can bounce you in the ball up and down, up and down. When Rita flies by she will—well, you know, maybe—stick to the trees or the house or, or maybe she could stick to the giant ball with you two in the middle. Er, nice to meet you."

Bobby looked at Bear Crimbo and Alfie Mouse's doubtful faces and said, "It's not a good plan, is it?"

"Well," said Alfie, "it would be if we had a hundred round-the-clocks."

Bear Crimbo stood up, straightened his shirt, took a sip of tea, and said, "I have a plan to guide Rita home safely. Bobby, I want you to make two of the longest pieces of silk string that you have ever made, okay?"

"Okay," said Bobby.

"What can I do?" asked Alfie Mouse.

Bear Crimbo smiled and said, "I need you to sew together four of my pocket hankies to make one big square, then attach two sticks at either end, okay?"

"Okay, right away," said Alfie. Then, to everyone's surprise, Bear Crimbo started to climb out the window.

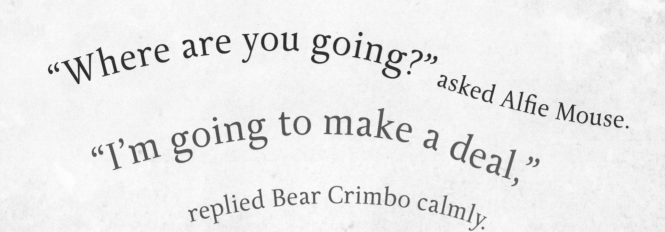

"Where are you going?" asked Alfie Mouse.

"I'm going to make a deal,"

replied Bear Crimbo calmly.

T. J. MEETS NOODLES

T. J. cut through the Great North Wind as if it were just a breeze. He had two things on his mind: he must get Crimbo's lovely letter to Santa, and he must get home in time for Christmas dinner. T. J. had to make enough pancakes for all of his new friends.

After walking against the Great North Wind for about four much morey hours, T. J. was covered in ice, so he stopped to shake it all off before continuing on his way. A short while later, T. J. touched his mouth and found that the little sequiny purse was not there. "Oh, no!" T. J. said in a complete panic. "No, no! Rita Robin is relying on me. She flies half way around the world, and I lose Crimbo's lovely letter!"

Just then he heard footsteps in the snow, really quick little steps—crunch, crunch, crunch, crunch. He took a look back and saw the funniest looking little birdie he'd ever seen, with big feet and stubby little wings. "Hello," T. J. said. "What's your name?"

"My name is Noodles. I overheard that you were going to Santa's Grotto, and I, er, I know Santa. He's my friend."

"I've never seen a bird like you before," T. J. laughed.

"Yeah, yeah, I know. See, er, I'm a penguin. I don't fly. I swim, and I swim well, too. I thought if I showed you a short cut to Santa's Grotto, the quicker we could get back for those Christmas pancakes."

"But I've lost my friend's sequiny purse, and I won't be able to give it to Santa even if you are his friend."

"Well, er," said Noodles, "is this it?"

"Yes!" sang T. J. with happiness. "Where did you find it?"

"When you did your shaky-shake thing back there to get rid of all the snow and ice, I saw it fall to the ground. I love it, all soft and shiny, but if it belongs to you then you can have it."

With that, because T. J. was so relieved, he jumped up and down so much it cracked the ice beneath T. J. and Noodles.

Noodles ran and climbed onto T. J., shouting, "Hang on! Here we go on a secret slide!" *WHOOSH!* And down they went into a beautiful ice tube, down, down, around and around.

T. J. shouted, "What is this?"

Noodles, loving every moment of the slippery slide, said, "This is the longer but quicker way to Santa's Grotto!"

After much morey minutes on the most fun slide in the world, they both came to a stop at a little red door. Noodles slowly opened it, and T. J. couldn't believe his eyes! Presents of all different shapes and sizes were wrapped in paper of every color imaginable, while hundreds of elves were making and wrapping presents and reading letters from all over the world.

"Hello, Noodles," said a very important-looking elf. "What can I do for you?"

"I need to see Santa," said Noodles.

The elf just laughed and said, "Santa can't see anyone. He is checking his sleigh and meeting with the head reindeer."

T. J. stood up as tall as he could and said, "I have a lovely letter from a bear friend of mine called Crimbo. This letter has been half-way around the world, with only love and hope to carry it. It's covered in the finest silk and holds the dream of a bear that believes Santa does not listen to bears."

"Well, why didn't you say so?" said the elf. "Follow me." T. J. and Noodles followed, wide-eyed, and walked through a big red and gold door. There, standing over a map of the world, was SANTA himself, with a perfect white beard and bright, rosy cheeks.

"Ho! Ho! Ho!" he laughed. "Where is this lovely letter from Bear Crimbo?"

T. J. almost asked how Santa already knew about the lovely letter, but then he remembered how he had heard that Santa had eyes and ears everywhere. He handed over the sequiny purse and said, "It's an honor to meet you, Sir."

"Ho! Ho! Ho! Just call me Santa!" Santa put on his glasses and started to unravel Bobby's silk. He would be the first person to actually read Bear Crimbo's lovely letter. And this is what it said:

Dear Santa,

I have written to you so many times without a response, so I have decided that this will be the last time that I'll ever write a lovely letter. But, just in case you do receive this, I would like, with all my heart, to tell you what I want for Christmas.

Santa, more than anything I would love what I see when sleepy-time takes me to the land of dreamies every night.

I don't know if it is possible, but I would love a HUG for Christmas, maybe even more than one.

I hope you can hear bears.

HAPPY CHRISTMAS,

LOVE

Bear
Crimbo

Santa pulled a hanky from his pocket and blew his red nose. He remembered hugging Bear Crimbo and giving him to Mrs. Flump for Christmas, many years before. That is what Bear Crimbo can see in his dreamies every night, but after years of living in the loft he no longer remembers..

Santa said calmly, "All bears need to be hugged and loved the whole year, not just at Christmas." Santa put the sequiny purse and lovely letter into his big red jacket pocket, then said to T. J. and Noodles, "Come on, you two. I have something amazing to show you!"

Santa took them to a big wooden treasure chest, which he unlocked with a golden key. A grey sack fell out. Santa picked the sack up as if it were priceless. He looked at T. J. and said with pride, "This, my big, fluffy friend, is the reason that Christmas can happen. No matter how many presents you put in this magic sack, you will never be able to fill it, and it will only ever grow to a certain size— so I can always carry it down everybody's chimneys."

Santa placed the old, grey sack under a big bronze funnel and pushed a button. Suddenly, thousands and thousands of presents poured into the magic sack! Then he continued his work.

Santa personally checked the bells on the reindeer while the elves made sure the sleigh was ready for the long night ahead. Santa then turned to T. J. and Noodles. "Come on," he said. "I'll drop you off at home. I hear you have fifty new friends coming over for pancake Christmas dinner."

They climbed into the sleigh. "Yah!" shouted Santa, and with the sound of sleigh bells CHRISTMAS HAD BEGUN.

CRIMBO AND THE KING OF THE FIREFLIES

Back on Plip Plop Road, the sun was feeling so sleepy.... Bear Crimbo was on his way to the Cherry Blossom Tree, inside of which the king of the fireflies, King Glowiest, lived. Bear Crimbo knocked three times on the tree and was instantly greeted by fifty fireflies, King Glowiest's finest guards.

"Who goes there?" asked the head guard.

"Bear Crimbo, sir."

"How can we help you?"

"I need to make a deal with King Glowiest, and we must hurry because the sun is nearly asleep."

With that said, the guards were gone. After a few much morey minutes, about five hundred fireflies surrounded the Cherry Blossom Tree. Then the head guard announced at the top of his voice, "We present King Glowiest!" Out flew the king of the fireflies.

Bear Crimbo bowed respectfully. "How can I help you, Bear Crimbo?" asked the king.

Bear Crimbo explained that the sun would be asleep soon and that his best friend, Rita Robin, would have no light to guide her safely home. "I have asked my friend Bobby Spider to make two strong silk strings, and Alfie Mouse is finishing a kite to go at the end of them. I need all of your fireflies to stand on the strings and glow as bright as they can, to make a bright road in the sky to bring my lovely friend home safely on this Christmas Eve. In return, I guarantee that, if you or any guards fall into a spider web, you will be released immediately. No spider will ever harm you or any of your subjects again."

A humming sound filled the air, then the king raised his hand. There was instant silence. "We would be honored to help you and your friends," said King Glowiest.

Bear Crimbo bowed again and replied, "I am so grateful. If there is anything I can do for you in the future, just let me know."

The king lowered his head respectfully, then snapped his fingers. All five hundred fireflies took hold of Bear Crimbo and lifted him up, up to the loft on Plip Plop Road. Bear Crimbo explained to Alfie Mouse and Bobby Spider the deal he had struck with King Glowiest, and they began to get their plan ready. The sun had gone to sleep by now. To get Rita home, their plan had to work.

RITA'S RETURN

An exhausted Rita Robin was very close to Plip Plop Road, but with so many lights of all different shapes, colors, and sizes, there was no way she could find her way home safely. In her heart, she knew Bear Crimbo had not forgotten about the light to guide her home, but she desperately needed to see it now. She flew around and around, hoping to see this beautiful little light. But there was nothing. She began to lose hope. She wanted so badly to see the ones she loved.

But Bear Crimbo was ready. With Alfie and Bobby's help, he lifted the kite to the window. As the wind blew, they let go. WHOOSH! Up went the kite with the breeze, the silk strings and hankies, stitched with so much love, holding strong and tight. At that moment, King Glowiest appeared and ordered his guards to march up each of the strings. Left, right, left, right they quickly moved up and up. As they did so, the most magical hum filled the air, as the fireflies beat their wings together. The king slowly raised his arms, and at that moment he and all the guards started to glow, golden and bright, like hundreds of tiny stars in the night, a road in the sky made of fireflies. The brightest light of all was King Glowiest himself, right in the middle of the window where the beeswax candle should have been.

Rita felt she might fall to the ground, but somehow she managed to look up one last time— and she could not believe her eyes!

She flew straight into the middle of the road of lights and was carried by the air from the beating wings of the fireflies, floating softly toward the window.

"Rita!" shouted Bear Crimbo.

"It's Rita!" sang Bobby and Alfie. Tears of joy fell from the three friends' eyes. Rita's heart was full of love. She couldn't believe that so much effort had gone into getting her home safely. She flapped her wings as hard as she could and shot into the arms of Bear Crimbo.

Bear Crimbo could feel Rita's beating heart. He put his arms around Alfie, Bobby, and Rita and said softly, "I've missed you, Rita! Friendship comes in all shapes and sizes, and I love all of you."

Then Rita thanked King Glowiest for his help. Bear Crimbo wanted to ask Rita all about her journey and, of course, his lovely letter, but he knew his friend needed to sleep. So he said to everyone, "It's Christmas morning tomorrow, and it's getting late. We must let Rita sleep." Bear Crimbo laid her upon an old cashmere blanket, but Rita was already sound asleep.

Alfie Mouse whispered, "Don't worry, B. C. I'm sure Santa has your lovely letter."

One by one the fireflies flew from the loft. As they did, each guard whispered, "Good night, sweet dreams, Miss Rita Robin." The beating of their wings sounded like the perfect lullaby. It wasn't long before all in Plip Plop Road were asleep.

But Bear Crimbo was dreaming that Christmas was nearly over and no one had mentioned his lovely letter or even said Merry Christmas to him. In his sleep, he started to cry, convinced that he would never meet Santa.

He was awakened by Bobby Spider, Alfie Mouse, and Rita Robin. "B. C., what's wrong?" they asked.

Sniffing and wiping his nose, Bear Crimbo was about to tell his friends about his dreamy, when a deep voice asked, "Why are you crying, Bear Crimbo?"

Bear Crimbo had never heard a voice so big. There, standing in front of him, with the most wonderful smile, was Santa himself! Bear Crimbo rubbed his eyes. YES! Santa was still standing right in front of him. "I thought I would never get to meet you, Santa. That means you got my lovely letter!"

"You have many friends who love you, Bear Crimbo," said Santa.

"And they have a bear who loves them too!" Crimbo replied.

"I believe this belongs to you," said Santa, handing the sequiny purse to Rita.

She took a deep breath and said, "Thank you."

Santa asked if they could all sit down. He took Bear Crimbo's lovely letter from his pocket, placed it on his knee, and put on his spectacles. "The first thing I want to say," said Santa, "is that I do listen to bears." Bear Crimbo smiled. "You wrote me a lovely letter, asking for a hug, maybe even more than one. I receive millions of letters each year full of wishes. Crimbo, I know someone else who needs a hug. In fact, there are thousands of little boys and girls all over the world who need love and hugs."

Santa smiled. "Bear Crimbo, you are a very special bear. I made you myself years ago and gave you to Mrs. Flump when she was a little girl. She used to hug you every day, and that is what you see in the land of dreamies. You remember being hugged."

Bear Crimbo wiped away a happy tear.

"There is something you should know, something I should have told you when I made you, Bear Crimbo. You are a bear that needs a hug for Christmas. And yet the thousands of children all over the world dream of being hugged by you. Yes, by you, Bear Crimbo! Even your name means Christmas. You are the Christmas Bear. I made you to give hugs. In return, you will always get one back. That is the Law of Hugs. So I have decided to give all of you a very special gift for Christmas."

With that, Santa sprinkled some magic dust onto the wall. Instantly, a beautiful little oak door appeared. "This door will only unlock itself once a year, after the stroke of midnight on Christmas morning," explained Santa. "Only you, Bear Crimbo, and your friends can go through this door. On the other side, you will be taken to a child who dreams of being hugged by you, Bear Crimbo—oh, and all your friends, of course!" laughed Santa. "It is there on Christmas Day, that *the Law of Hugs* will be put into place—because of you, Bear Crimbo. But remember, Plip Plop Road is where you live. The door is *only* to be used very early on Christmas morning."

Santa stood, then said, "Before I leave, would you do something for me?"

"Anything!" said Bear Crimbo.

"Well, I wondered if you would give me a hug." Bear Crimbo instantly ran and stretched his arms around Santa, squeezing as hard as he could. Then Rita Robin, Bobby Spider, and Alfie Mouse all hugged Santa as well.

As the sun slowly began to wake up on Christmas morning, this one big hug created the most powerful feeling, a moment made purely by friendship.

Santa, who didn't like goodbyes very much, blew his red nose and said, "Bear

Crimbo, I will see you next Christmas for my hug." Then Santa gave Rita a necklace, Bobby a bracelet, and jacket pins for Alfie and Crimbo. All were engraved, "SANTA'S HELPER."

Suddenly, a red glow appeared from outside the window. "We must hurry home to the North Pole," said a voice from outside. The friends could see a reindeer.

"I am late for a pancake dinner!" laughed Santa.

"Pancakes?" said Bear Crimbo, looking confused.

"Ho! Ho! Ho!" Santa laughed. "Rita will explain. Well, see you next year." With a whoosh, up he went into the night sky.

Bear Crimbo was tingling all over. "Merry Christmas," he said.

"Merry Christmas to you, B. C.," his friends replied. It was the morning of Christmas, and Bear Crimbo was with the ones he loved—and that was the best gift of all.

Bear Crimbo carefully put Santa's pin into the lapel of his jacket, then turned to his friends and said, "Let's put the Law of Hugs into action." Rita flew onto Bear Crimbo's shoulder. Alfie climbed into Crimbo's jacket pocket, and Bobby hung on by a silk thread.

Then, not knowing where in the world the magic door would take them, *Bear* Crimbo turned the little golden handle and walked through. . . .

My *lovely* letter

Civility costs nothing. — M. W. GOSS

About the author:

Matt Goss wrote the story of *Bear Crimbo* to bring love, warmth, and kindness into every home for Christmas. The story reinforces the importance of values, family, and friendship for today's children.

Matt Goss has enjoyed more than a decade of success as a singer and entertainer. As a musical artist, he has sold more than 16 million albums worldwide, including 13 Top Five singles.

Matt is consistently a sold-out headliner in Las Vegas at the world famous Caesar's Palace. He continues to write songs for the stage and high-profile recording artists like Keri Hilson and Akon. His best-selling autobiography, *More Than You Know*, was published in 2005. *Gossy*, his most recent album, available on iTunes, was released in September 2009.

In 2010, Matt played Royal Albert Hall in London and had his song "Lovely Las Vegas" named as the official theme song of NASCAR.

He is currently at the top of the charts in England, featured on the single "Firefly," a collaboration with Paul Oakenfold, the superstar producer of electronica music.

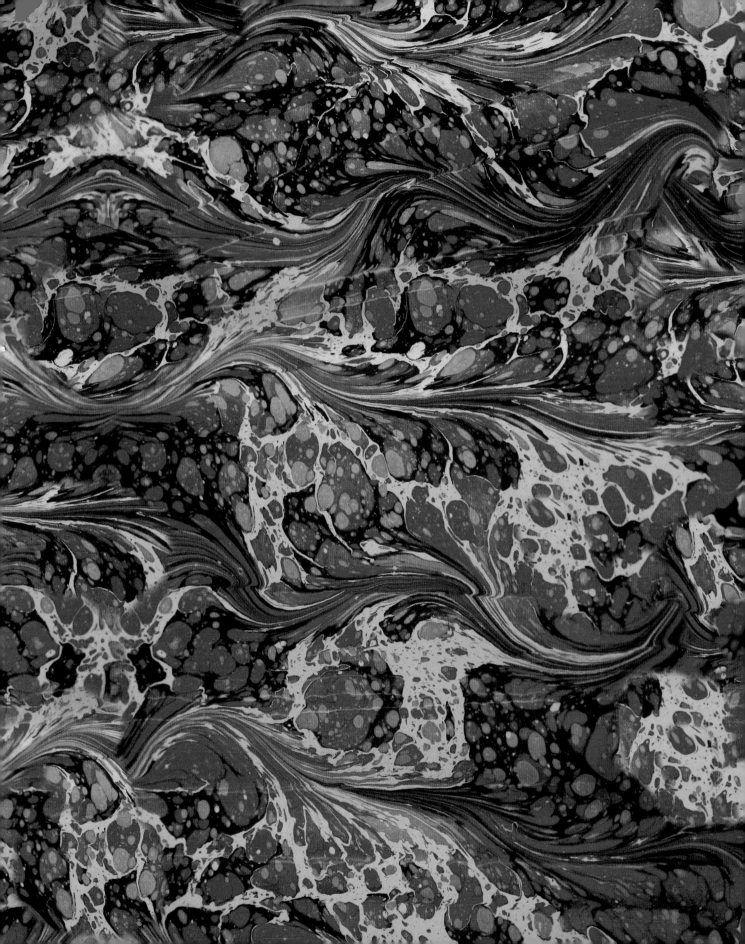

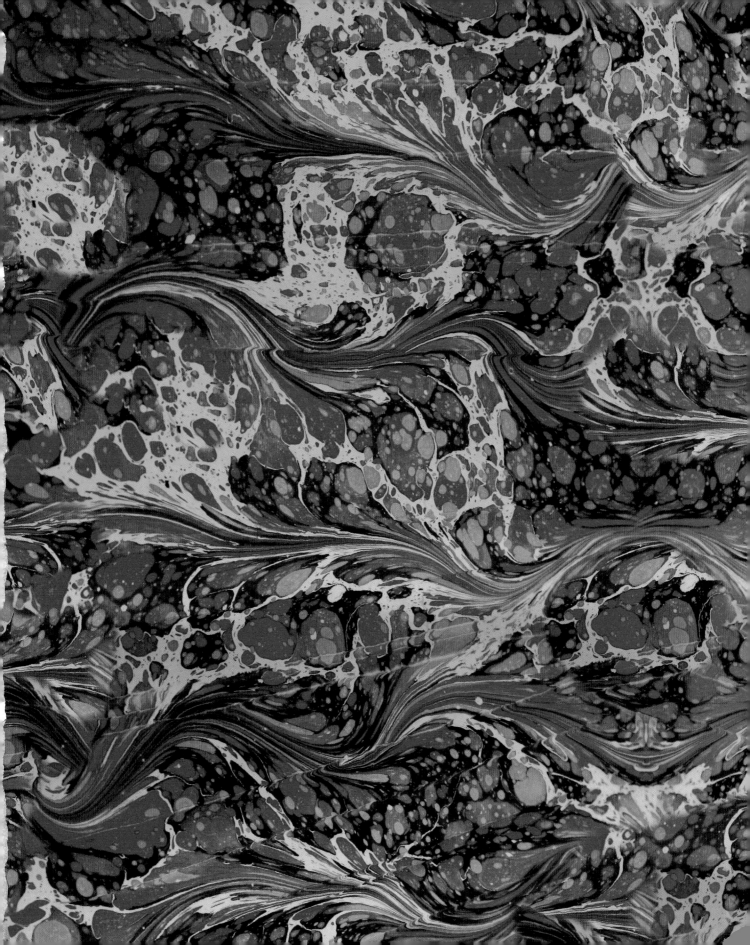

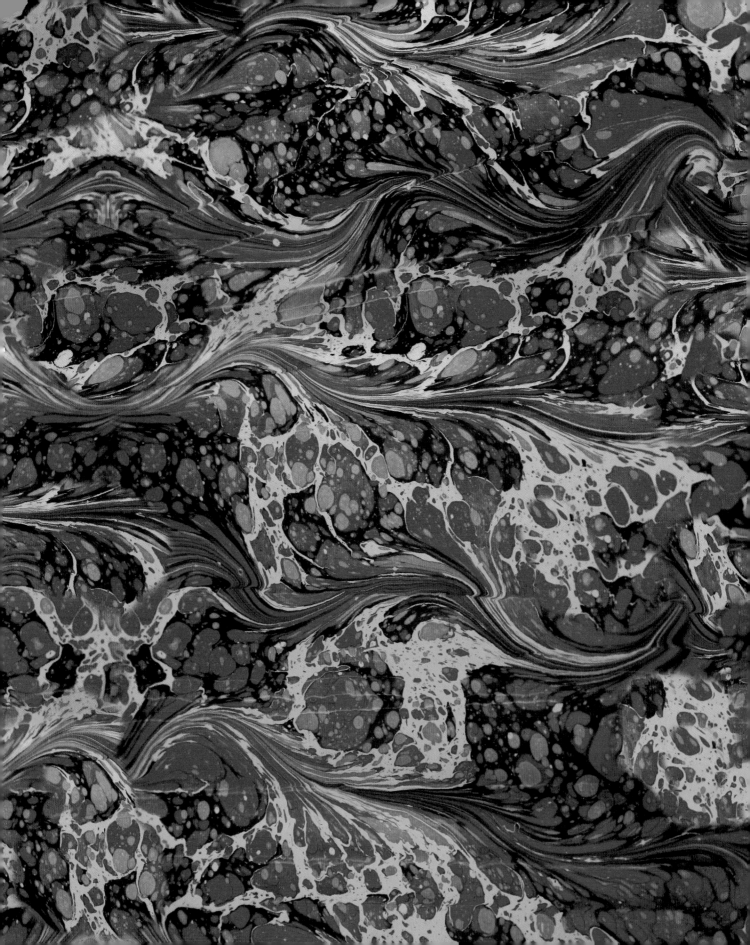

Published by Hilton Publishing Company, Inc.
816 Fort Wayne Avenue, Indianapolis, IN 46204
317-602-8090
www.hiltonpub.com
Copyright ©2008, 2010 Matt Goss

Library of Congress Cataloging-in-Publication Data
 Goss, Matt, 1968-
    Bear Crimbo / written by Matt Goss.
       p. cm.
    ISBN 978-0-9815381-3-6
    [1. Teddy bears—Fiction. 2. Toys—Fiction. 3. Animals—Fiction. 4. Letters—Fiction. 5. Santa Claus—Fiction.] I. Title.
    PZ7.G6792Be 2009
    [Fic]—dc22

                          2008018598

Grant E. Mabie, Managing Editor
Melanie Florio, Illustrations
Laura Klynstra, Design
Richard McLaren, Author photograph

Printed in the United States

10   11   12   13   14   15   16 / ❖ /   06   05   04   03   02